Finding a Home

By C.S. CROOK

Carolyn Sue Crook. <u>Finding a Home</u>

ISBN-13: 978-1500945091

ISBN-10: 1500945099

This is a heartwarming nature series about a little boy who longs for a dog of his own and an elderly man who is forced to give up his beloved pet. Johnny moves from the desert of West Texas to the West Coast fishing village, Fort Bragg, California, and has to leave behind dear friends and his only pet a horned toad. Just up the road from Johnny's new home, he discovers a scary looking dilapidated old house. There he finds an elderly, grumpy man who has a dog named Trouble. The man tries to scare Johnny away, but Johnny does not scare easily. Later in,' Johnny's Heroic Adventure', Johnny goes back to visit the elderly man and realizes that something is very wrong. The man's dog is straining against its chain and barking wildly at the house. Later in 'The Magic Wishbone', Hazel, one of Johnny's new friends, makes a wish for the first time ever on Thanksgiving Day, with her mother using a magic wishbone. She refuses to say what she wished for and insists that the magic needs time to happen, although she doesn't understand exactly how magic works. In 'Johnny's Treasure Adventure', Johnny and his friends help to solve a mystery which spans beyond a century, when they find buried treasure near the beach. Together, with the help of the police department, they find answers for how the treasure wound up where it did and who it belonged to. But there is one piece of jewelry in the treasure chest that turns out to have a ghost attached to it. The ghost makes it frighteningly clear that no one else is to have the ruby necklace. This series is about friendships and difficult decisions. It is also about family and how hard it is to move away from dear friends. Step into Johnny's world and follow him on his adventures where the wildlife and scenery comes vividly alive. This series is packed with action and drama, but most of all, it about people caring about and for one another. In this series you will find horned toads, rattlesnakes, raccoons, birds, ponies, fish and a slug, which are all a good mix for children with inquisitive minds.

There are six books in 'Johnny's Adventure' series. #1 'Johnny's Reptile Adventure', #2 'The Skipper's Captain', #3 'Johnny's Heroic Adventure', #4 'Finding A Home', #5 'The Magic Wishbone', and #6 'Johnny's Treasure Adventure'.

For Bill, the love of my life.

For Sean and Vanessa, our amazing children.

For all of whom have always encouraged and believed in me.

Contents

Chapter 1

When they pulled into the little parking area, Hank got out and opened the door for Lilly. He offered his hand and she took it. She stepped down from the truck and Johnny jumped down behind her. Hank then reached into the bed of the truck and took out two flashlights. He handed one to Lilly and the other to Johnny. He then reached back into the bed of the truck and took out a small cooler, which had a large blanket folded neatly on top.
"We're going to have a picnic?" Johnny asked, happily.

"We are, kind of," Hank replied. Hank nodded toward the beach and said, "Shall we?"

Johnny and Lilly switched on their flashlights and the three of them headed toward the water. When they reached the beach, Johnny could make out a large pile of something in the beam of his light. "What is that?" Johnny asked hesitantly, and then stopped in his tracks.

Hank laughed and said, "That is going to be a bonfire."

"What is a bonfire?" Johnny wanted to know.

"You, my young man, are about to find out."

When they approached, what Johnny could now see was a large pile of driftwood, and he saw a much smaller pile nearby. "My, you have been busy."

"That I have, but all for a good cause." Hank set the cooler down near the smaller pile of wood. He unfolded the blanket, pulled out some newsprint and kneeled down next to the small pile of driftwood. Sheet by sheet, he wadded it into loose balls and strategically tucked them into the belly of the woodpile. He then lit some of the paper in the smaller pile with a wooden match, and fanned the flame.

Johnny looked in awe at the larger pile and asked, "Hank, why are you even bothering to light that little one? You have this huge pile right here."

"I have to get this one started first, Johnny, so the coals can die down. I'm going to cook dinner on it."

"Oh, like we did back home with Grandpa," Johnny said, and looked at Lilly over the small fire that Hank had started. He could see his mother nod at him in the flickering light. When Hank was satisfied that the fire was going well, he moved to the larger pile. "Can I help you, Hank, with this one?"

"Sure you can, Johnny. Here, take some of these." Hank handed Johnny some of the paper. Johnny followed Hank's lead and crumpled up the sheets of paper into balls. He then stuck them, one by one, as far into the pile that his little arms would reach. When they had used up all the paper, Hank smiled and said, "Now is the fun part." Hank started on the water side and walked slowly around the pile, lighting all the paper balls that were near the bottom. A soft breeze had picked up, coming in off the water. It fanned the flames nicely for Hank, only occasionally blowing out his match. Hank stood back and studied his handiwork. Small flames licked up from the belly of the fire and turned into larger ones. There was a loud pop from the fire which made Lilly jump. Her two companions laughed at the sight and she joined in with them. The flames grew larger and hissed, as they sent sparks into the sky.

"Wow, that is some fire," Lilly said in admiration.

Hank grinned proudly and asked, "Do you two think this will keep us warm?"

"It will keep us nice and toasty," Johnny said. "What are you making for dinner, Hank? I'm starving."

"Johnny, where are your manners?" Lilly scolded him.

"Oh, that's quite alright, Lilly. The fact of the matter is I'm starving too. Well, on the menu tonight, for starters, is pickled shrimp and the main course is steak."

Johnny giggled and said, "He sounds like Rudy, doesn't he Mommy?"

"I don't know about him sounding like Rudy, but I do know the food sounds just delicious."

"How come you're not fixing the fish that we caught?" Johnny asked.

Lilly said, "Now, Johnny, that is just rude!"

"I eat my fair share of fish and then some. I thought that I would take a break from that tonight, with the exception of the shrimp."

"Johnny, you tell him that you are sorry."

Johnny looked down at the sand and dug the toe of his shoe into it. He mumbled, "I'm sorry."

"No, Johnny, you look him straight in the eye and say it loud enough that we can all hear it."

Johnny lifted his chin and looked Hank in the eyes. "I'm sorry, Hank."

"Thank you, Captain, apology accepted."

Lilly took the blanket and let the breeze help her spread it out upon the sand. "Do you think this spot is good?" she asked Hank.

"I think that will be just fine. If we get too warm, we can always move it back a bit." Hank took plates out of the ice cooler and set them on the blanket. He then placed some silverware and folded napkins on top of the plates. Then he placed a jar of pickled shrimp next to the plates, went over to the small fire, stirred the hot coals with a stick and spread them out. Lilly watched him and had a sudden pang of homesickness. She fondly remembered Grandpa doing this same thing countless times. She wondered how they were all doing. She missed them so much. Hank placed a metal grate upon the rocks that rimmed the fire and laid the steak on top. The steak sizzled and small rogue flames darted up from the hot embers. Very soon, the steak gave off a tantalizing aroma.

3

Lilly stood with her back to the bonfire and continued to watch Hank. "Can I do anything to help you?" she asked.

"I've got everything under control, you two are my guests."

"Wow, did you hear that?" Johnny asked them.

"Hear what?" Lilly asked.

"My tummy growled as loudly as a bear."

"I will soon have enough food to feed you and the bear inside you," Hank told him.

Johnny laughed. "You are funny, Hank!" Hank just shrugged his shoulders and took a loaf of bread and a cold vegetable salad from the cooler.

Lilly looked at the impressive spread and asked Hank, "You made all that?"

"I made everything except the bread."

"I am impressed!" she said.

"Don't say that until you taste it all but, just so you know, that is my goal, to impress you."

"It doesn't matter how it all tastes. You have already accomplished your goal."

"Of course it matters how it tastes, Mommy!"

Hank laughed and said, "You see what I told you, Lilly, that boy of yours is smart."

When the steak was done, Hank said, "Well, let's see what you two think." He put the steak on one of the plates and set it on the blanket, next to the salad. Hank then sat down cross legged upon the blanket and indicated for them to join him. Johnny and Lilly picked their places across from Hank.

Hank took up a carving knife, sliced the steak and passed it to Lilly first. Lilly put a few slices upon Johnny's plate, before she served herself. "This smells so good," she said to Hank, as she passed him back the plate. "Are those red bell peppers that I see in the shrimp?"

"Yes, it is a dish that my mother used to always make. She was forever finding creative ways to make the same stuff taste like something new. In our case, that would be seafood."

"I can't wait to try them, they look so delicious," Lilly told him.

Hank picked up the jar, took off the lid and handed the jar to Lilly. "Then, I say, wait no longer, this is your night."

Lilly blushed and took the jar. "Thank you."

"Can I try some too? I have never tried shrimp before," Johnny said.

"Of course you can," Lilly said, and put a generous spoonful of shrimp on his plate.

Johnny popped one into his mouth right away. "Yep, Hank, they sure are good." Lilly put some on her plate and handed the jar back to Hank.

"Thank you, Johnny," Hank told him, as he passed out the rest of the meal.

Lilly waited until Hank picked up his fork and knife, before she tasted anything. When she tasted a little of everything, she dabbed her mouth daintily with her napkin and said, "Hank, this is amazing."

"Do you really think so?"

"I do."

"Well then, eat up!" Hank said proudly.

After they finished their meal, they moved over to the bonfire. The flames illuminated their faces in the dark. Lilly asked, "Hank, have you always been a fisherman? I guess that is a silly question, because you learned it growing up from your dad."

"No, it is not silly at all. The fact of the matter is I haven't. While it is true that I learned the trade and how to operate The Skipper growing up, I wasn't grown up until after I joined the Navy."

"Wow, you were a sailor?" Johnny asked.

"I was a frogman."

"What is a frogman?" Johnny wanted to know.

"It is the job that I did for the Navy. Mostly, I wore wetsuits and swam around the shorelines of other counties."

"Why did you do that?" Johnny asked.

"I can't tell you, because it is classified information."

"What does classified information mean?" Johnny asked.

Lilly answered the question, "It means that he can't tell you."

Hank continued, "Sadly, while I was deployed, Mom wrote to tell me that Dad had passed away and, before my tour was done, she was gone too. All that was left was The Skipper and the house when I was able to return home."

"Hank, I'm so sorry to hear that," Lilly said softly.

Hank shrugged and said, "They had me late in life. They always said I was a miracle child. I was the only one that they could have. They were good folks."

"What about you Lilly? Do you still have your parents?"

"No, they are gone too."

"I'm sorry to hear that. Do you have any brothers or sisters?"

"No, just like you, I was the only one. Growing up, I had friends who had huge families, so I was never lonely. I guess I just never knew what I was missing when I was younger."

Hank smiled at her and said, "Yeah, it was pretty much that way with me too."

"I'm tired, Mommy," Johnny said.

"I'm sorry," Hank said, "I've had you folks out here way too late."

"No, we've had a very lovely day, Hank, and your meal was wonderful."

"Let me just gather this stuff up and I will get the two of you back to your car," Hank said.

"Let me help you," Lilly said.

Lilly helped Hank pack up, while Johnny enjoyed the last flames of the bonfire. When they walked back up to the truck, the bonfire was nothing but dying embers. They rode together back to the harbor, to where Lilly had parked her car. Hank pulled up next to her car and helped her out of the truck.

"It will take me just a minute to fetch your fish that you two caught today," Hank said. Hank dashed over to his boat and soon returned with one very large package and a much smaller one. He handed them to Lilly and said, "I think those give you both bragging rights."

Lilly smiled up at him, took the packages and placed them on the back seat of the Ford. She then turned back, looked up at him again and said, "Hank, I would like to thank you for the wonderful afternoon and evening."

He took one of her hands in his and kissed it. "The pleasure was mine," he said, as he released her hand.

She blushed prettily and said to Johnny, "You need to give that hat back to Hank, because it is very special to him. His poppa gave it to him."

7

Reluctantly, Johnny took the captain's hat off his head and handed it to Hank.

Hank took it and said, "Until next time, Captain."

Johnny perked up and he said, "You mean we get to go out on the Skipper with you again?"

Chapter 2

"Sure, you can, if you would like too," Hank said, and shot a sideways glance at Lilly.

"Like to, I would love to!" Johnny looked over at his mother and said, "Can we go again sometime, Mommy?"

"We would both love to, Hank."

Hank smiled broadly and said, "Then, I reckon that is settled."

"Well, goodnight Hank and thank you once again," Lilly said. Then to Johnny she said, "Into the car, Captain." Johnny shot a grin in Hank's direction and obeyed his mother.

Hank stood in the deepening darkness and watched as the Ford's headlights carefully navigated their way up the steep, winding hill and back out of the harbor. He felt more alive this night then he could ever remember.

Before retiring to their cabin, Johnny and Lilly dropped the fish off at the lodge. Johnny told Howard all about his fishing experience, while Lilly placed the fish into the walk-in refrigerator. When she joined them, Howard said to her, "This young man of yours tells me that you caught yourself a beauty?"

"Yes, I was pretty lucky. I guess I had a good teacher."

"Well, Hank is certainly the man to learn how to fish from. His family has been earning a living off the sea for generations. What are you going to do with it?"

"I thought that I would give it to Molly tomorrow. She has such a large family and she is kind enough to watch Johnny for me next Saturday evening."

"Oh, is that so?" Howard asked.

Lilly realized that she had already said too much. "Yes," she said, and left it at that.

"Mommy is going to cook my fish up for my dinner tomorrow night," Johnny told him.

"That's not necessary, Lilly, I will be happy to do the honors. Just consider it a big thank you for helping me out of my jam last night."

"Alright, Howard, thank you. We will see you tomorrow night, then. Goodnight."

"Goodnight to you both," Howard said, and turned back to his grill.

Exhausted from the day in the sun, Johnny and Lilly returned to their cabin and were both soon fast asleep.

The next morning, when Lilly got to work, she walked up to the large tables in the back of the kitchen, where Molly was already busy prepping the fruit and vegetables for the day. "Good morning, Molly."

Molly looked up and said, "Top of the morning to you, Miss Lilly."

"I caught a large salmon yesterday, while we were out fishing with Hank and I was wondering if you would like it for your family?"

"My family loves to eat salmon. We would be very grateful to have it."

"Well, I'm very grateful that you are watching Johnny for me and on your day off to boot."

"Oh, Johnny will be no trouble. He is a joy to have around. My girls will fuss over him like mother hens who have had their eggs mixed about."

The visual image made Lilly laugh. "Well, when you get off of work, it is wrapped in the white paper on the shelf, just to the left of the door when you walk into the refrigerator."

"Thank you, I will remember it for sure, Miss Lilly. Did Johnny catch a fish? I know he was so very excited about the possibility."

"He did, and I'm sure that you are going to hear all about it this morning, when he comes in for breakfast."

Molly laughed and said, "In that case, I know that I will."

"I've got to go get into my uniform. I'll talk to you later, Molly."

"Yes, you scoot along, lass."

Later that morning, Doc stopped by the lodge for breakfast. He greeted Lilly with a huge smile when he saw her. "I have some great news for Johnny," he said.

"Mr. Thornton is better?" She asked hopefully.

"He is out of the intensive care unit and can have visitors for short periods. He is still pretty weak."

Lilly's face lit up, making her even more beautiful, Doc thought. "That is wonderful news. Is it alright if we go to visit him this afternoon?" she asked.

"It will be fine," Doc said.

"I can hardly wait to let Johnny know."

"He is very grumpy, though," Doc warned.

Lilly nodded. "I've got to get back to work, Mark," she said, and flashed him a smile before returning to the kitchen.

When Johnny woke up, he got himself dressed and went over to take care of Trouble. That was just becoming part of his everyday routine. It was also becoming the part of his day that he enjoyed the most, except when he got to go play with his friends. As usual, Trouble seemed just as happy to see him. "Is it me that you're happy to see, or just the food that I give you?" Trouble responded by wagging his tail faster. "Okay, you say it's a little bit of both. For your honesty, I will take you for a walk after breakfast." To Johnny's surprise, Trouble barked enthusiastically. "I think you are starting to understand what the words, 'Go for a walk,' mean." Trouble barked and lunged against his chain. "Okay, okay, we will go, just as soon as I get back." Johnny fed and watered the dog and gave him a quick scratch on top of his head. Johnny turned and walked down the drive. Trouble whimpered, as he watched Johnny go.

Johnny walked through one of the big doors into the lodge. Jo Lynn was there to greet him. "Good morning, Johnny," she said. Her bright, blue eyes seemed to twinkle even brighter this morning. "I think your mother has some wonderful news for you."

"She does?" Johnny asked, perplexed.

"Yes, she does."

"What is it?"

Jo Lynn motioned toward the kitchen in a graceful way and said, "You will have to go find out."

Johnny walked through the swinging doors and Gus's smile seemed to be bigger and happier as he said, "Lilly, look who is here."

Lilly looked over and saw Johnny. She set an order of pancakes up into the window, under the heat lamps, and came over to Johnny. "Doc came in this morning and said Mr. Thornton is better now. He said that we can go and visit him this afternoon, right after I get off of work, if you want too."

"Yes, I want to go. I have so much to tell him. Trouble and I have really missed him."

"Well, I'm sure that he will be happy to see you," Lilly said, and kissed him on the cheek.

"Gus, I caught a fish yesterday. It was a real fighter, even Hank said so."

"You did? What kind of fish was it?" Gus asked.

"I forget what it was." Johnny looked over at his mother. "Do you remember, Mommy?"

"Hank said that it was a perch."

"Oh, those are a lot of fun to catch. Hank is right, they are great fighters," Gus said.

"I was afraid that I had a shark on my line."

Gus laughed, and then saw by Johnny's face that he was serious. Gus straightened up his face and asked, "Were you scared?"

"Heck no, not even a little bit. I think I'm going to be a fisherman when I grow up." Johnny then asked his mother, "What is for breakfast?"

"You can have some scrambled eggs and toast, with fruit."

"Okay, I'm going to go and see Molly now," Johnny said. While Johnny waited for his breakfast, he told Molly all about his day fishing. One thing about Molly was that she was a great listener.

Johnny finished with his breakfast and took Trouble for his walk. There were a couple of guests from the lodge walking in the meadow. They were an elderly man and woman. They hesitated to walk past Johnny and Trouble. "Is that dog of yours going to bite us, sonny?" The elderly gentleman asked.

"Heck no, he is just as friendly as they come. He will even let you pet him."

The elderly lady spoke up, "You had best not, Martin that dog might be protective of the boy."

Carefully, the couple walked around Johnny and Trouble, giving them as wide a berth as they could. Johnny and Trouble went well beyond the eucalyptus trees on their walk. He didn't have to be back until lunch, so together they enjoyed the morning. After lunch, Johnny took his sled and went to the hill. He was disappointed to see that there were no children on the hill that day. He made the most out of the sunny afternoon and slid down the hill time and again, alone. Soon, he heard voices on the trail. He could tell that it was his friends, because he could make out Leslie's high, shrill voice. He left his sled on the hill and ran to meet them on the path.

"Where have you guys been? I've been waiting for hours."

Hazel was the first to speak up. "One of the stores in town was having a back to school sale today, so some of our parents made us go to try on some clothes."

Donna said, "I asked Mommy if we could go to the sale, because I need some new clothes. She said that we couldn't afford it."

Hazel said, "I have some things that I have grown out of; some real pretty things, Donna. I know my mother will let me give them to you, if I ask her."

Donna's face brightened up. "You would do that for me?"

"Of course I would," Hazel told her.

"Those would be hand-me-downs," Leslie smirked. "I only wear new clothes."

Bobby came quickly to Donna's defense. "No one cares what you wear, Leslie. I wear Fred's hand-me-downs every year and I'm glad to have them."

"That's because your family is poor," Leslie snapped back at him.

"Daddy says that as long as we have each other, a good roof over our heads, and something in our tummies when we go to bed at night, we are blessed."

"Come on, let's go ride our sleds," Fred said, and raced toward the hill. All the children raced after him.

While they were standing in line, Johnny told everyone that he was going to see his friend at the hospital.

Hazel asked, "Will he get to come home soon?"

"I sure hope so, because I miss him, and I know that Trouble misses him too."

"Are you going to bring Trouble here sometime, so we can see him?" she asked.

"Sure, I can do that. Maybe I can do that tomorrow."

"That would be fun. I like dogs." She smiled at him.

"I don't like dogs," Leslie whined.

"Nobody cares, Leslie," Bobby said, as he mounted his sled and awaited his turn. When Donna had reached the bottom of the hill and picked up her sled, he took off on his.

Lester piped up and said, "She's afraid of dogs."

"I am not! I just don't like them."

"You are too!" Lester said.

Leslie was happy to let it drop. She noticed the other children smiling and was happy that they didn't say anything. She was going to tell on Lester when she got home. That would teach him to make fun of her.

The other children were still playing, when Johnny had to leave. He wanted to make sure that he had plenty of time to feed and water Trouble. Most of all, he was excited to get to see Mr. Thornton. Johnny took one last turn on his sled and, when he picked it up, he looked back up the hill and waved goodbye to all his friends at the top. Hazel was on her sled poised for a takeoff. Reluctantly, he headed home. It confused him as to why, out of all his new friends, it was her that he was the happiest to see.

Chapter 3

After Johnny took care of the dog, he washed up a bit while he waited for his mother to get off of work. He went outside, set down on the front steps and twiddled his thumbs while he felt the minutes crawl by. Finally, he could see his mother walking toward him in the distance and he ran to meet her.

"I've been waiting and waiting for you to get off of work."

"You have?"

"Yes, I can hardly wait to go see Mr. Thornton."

"Well then, I won't take but a minute to freshen up before we go."

When they reached the cabin, Johnny walked up to the old Ford, pulled open the door on the passenger side and said, "I'll wait in here."

Lilly smiled and went inside the cabin. Soon, she reemerged and they were on their way to town at last. When they reached the hospital, Emily greeted them with a warm smile and stood up from behind her desk. "Hello, Doc said that I could be expecting to see the two of you. Please let me show you the way to Mr. Thornton's room."

"Is he expecting us?" Lilly asked.

"No, Doc wanted it to be a surprise for him. He thought that it would cheer him up, because he has had no other visitors." They walked down a long corridor with rooms on either side until; finally, Emily stopped and tapped on a door that was slightly ajar. "Yoo-hoo, Mr. Thornton, you have visitors." Without waiting for a reply she stepped back and motioned for them to go inside.

Johnny, smiling broadly, barged in ahead of his mother. "Surprise, Mr. Thornton!"

Finding a Home

"Who let you in here? How did you track me down?" Lilly stepped into the room after Johnny. Mr. Thornton eyed Lilly up and down, "Now this pretty lady is a surprise. Where did you find her for me, Johnny?"

"You're funny, Mr. Thornton, this is my mother."

"Well, why didn't you tell me that you had such a pretty momma?"

Lilly walked up beside his bed and extended her hand to him. "I'm Lilly, Mr. Thornton, and I'm very pleased to meet you, at last."

His large hand engulfed hers as he shook her hand and said, "You're not more pleased than I am to meet you. How is it that such a looker like you had such an ugly duckling?" Shocked, Lilly didn't know how to respond.

"I look like my daddy."

"Well then, that explains it," Mr. Thornton said.

"Hey, Doc says that I saved your life."

"Why did you go and do a fool thing like that?"

"I did it because you are my friend that is why. Trouble and I can't wait for you to come back home. I have been taking really good care of him. I have even been taking him on walks every morning."

"I can't wait to come home too. The food in this place is awful. They think that a bowl of Jell-O is a meal."

"Hey, guess what?" Johnny asked Mr. Thornton.

"I don't know what, I give up."

"Trouble has learned to bark, so he is not a worthless dog after all."

"You don't say? When did he learn that?"

"The first time that I heard him bark was the day that he helped me save your life. Then he figured out what the words, 'Go for a walk,' mean. He gets so excited when I say them that he barks."

"He must like going for those walks with you, I reckon."

"He does. We have a lot of fun together. Did you know that he is a great hunter?"

"No, I did not know that. We have not had the opportunity to do any hunting."

"His favorite thing is to flush quail out of the brush."

"He does that for you, does he?"

"Yes sir, he does, and he is dang good at it."

"Well you're plumb tuckering me out with all of this gibberish."

"Johnny, I think we had better let Mr. Thornton rest now," Lilly said softly.

"Okay, we will come back and see you just as soon as we can, Mr. Thornton," Johnny said to his friend, and then Johnny and Lilly turned to leave.

Mr. Thornton said, "Johnny, thank you for taking such good care of Trouble, and also for saving my life, I guess."

Johnny turned back around and said, "I'm happy that I still have you, Mr. Thornton. You sure gave me a scare, and I like taking care of Trouble for you."

"It was nice to have met you, Mr. Thornton," Lilly said.

"It is always nice to meet a pretty lady. You come back and leave him at home."

Lilly smiled and said, "Get some rest now." Johnny and Lilly left the room.

Johnny and Lilly passed by Emily's desk on their way out of the hospital. "Oh, you're done with your visit so soon? How was it?" Emily wanted to know.

Lilly smiled sweetly at her and said, "It was lovely."

Emily smiled back at her, knowingly, and said, "I will see you two the next time you come in." Johnny gave her a little wave goodbye and Lilly simply nodded, and they headed for home.

On the way, Johnny asked, "Aren't we going to the beach tonight?"

Lilly glanced over at him and said, "Do you mind if we don't? I just feel like I need to rest a bit before we have dinner."

"No, I don't mind. I got to see my friend."

"Your friend doesn't seem very friendly most of the time."

"Oh, you've just got to get to know him. That is his way. He tries to scare people off."

"Well, I bet that he does a pretty good job of that."

"He liked you, Mommy."

Lilly smiled and said, "I suppose he did." They pulled up in front of their cabin and went inside. "I'm going to just lie down for a bit before dinner," she told Johnny and kicked off her shoes and lay down on her bed. Johnny took off his shoes, climbed onto her bed, and laid down beside her. She kissed him on the forehead and together they fell fast asleep. Dinner was forgotten.

Johnny awoke, just as the day was breaking. He looked around the cabin, through a sleepy fog. He realized that he was still dressed in his clothes from the day before and he was in his mother's bed. Confused, he looked around the room. The cabin was quiet. He sat up in the bed, rubbed the sleep from his eyes, and suddenly realized that he was about to wet himself. He bounded off the bed and made a beeline for the bathroom. He was wide awake now. He knew that his mother was already at work and she would not be expecting him this early in the morning, but he was starving. He ran a wet wash cloth over his face and put on his jacket. Normally, he would tend to Trouble first before eating himself, but Trouble was used to eating a little bit later, so Johnny stepped out onto the front porch and took a deep breath of the crisp morning air. The fog was blanketing the meadow like thick smoke and the trees behind the meadow stood dark and ominous, as the early morning sun lit the eastern sky well behind them.

Johnny stepped off the porch and started his trek to the lodge. He could not help but to imagine what critters prowled for food, concealed under the blanket of fog. As Johnny approached the lodge, he saw Doc's car sitting in the parking lot. Johnny stepped up his pace, because he was eager to get to talk to Doc about his visit with Mr. Thornton.

Jo Lynn greeted him at the door. "What an early bird you are this morning, Johnny."

Johnny looked up at her and smiled. "Yep, I am an early bird," he said, and headed for the end of the bar, where Doc was sitting and having his breakfast. "Good morning, Doc."

"Well this is an unexpected surprise to see you here at this ungodly hour in the morning. How are you Johnny?"

"I'm just fine, Doc. We got to see Mr. Thornton at the hospital yesterday."

"Yes, he told me that you were there."

"He did?" Johnny asked surprised.

"Yes, he did. He told me that we needed to hire some nurses that looked like your mother."

"Why?" Johnny asked, in confused innocence.

Doc laughed, he could not help himself. "Mr. Thornton thinks that she is pretty."

"Oh," Johnny replied, and thought of Hazel. "I wanted to say thank you for taking such good care of my friend."

"You are welcome. It has been an experience for me for sure, but I'm glad that he is doing better."

"He doesn't like the food though."

Doc said, "No one has ever been known to like hospital food. I think that they make it taste that way so everyone will want to hurry up and get well."

"Oh, I didn't know that," Johnny said thoughtfully.

Doc smiled and added, "It makes us doctors look good when they get well so fast."

"Don't they get well so fast because you are a good doctor?"

"I'd like to think so." Doc smiled at him and downed the last bit of his coffee.

As if on cue, Jo Lynn magically appeared with a pot of freshly brewed coffee. "Would you like more coffee, Doc?"

"No thanks, Jo Lynn. I've got to get going."

"We are going to come and see him again, just as soon as we can," Johnny said.

"Well, maybe I will get to see the two of you there," Doc said, as he paid his bill, and then he left.

Johnny walked through the swinging doors into the kitchen. Gus looked up from his work and gave Johnny a big grin. Lilly stood beside Gus at the grill. She wiped her forehead with the back of her hand and looked over at Johnny. "Are you starving?"

"I sure am starving."

"Okay, what do you say that you start with some of Gus's famous johnnycakes?"

"I was hoping that you would say that! They are my favorite." Gus gave him another grin.

"You go on back and I'll bring you some cocoa," Lilly said.

Johnny could tell that this was going to be a great day. He walked around the bank of ovens and found Molly, busily chopping away.

"Good morning, Molly."

Molly looked up at him and smiled. "Top of the morning to you, Johnny. I understand that you are going to be coming over to my house this Saturday evening?"

"That is what Mom said."

"My two girls are going to make a big fuss over you for sure."

Johnny was not sure if he liked the way that sounded, but he didn't say anything. He walked over to the table in the corner and sat down to wait for his breakfast. Johnny realized that he didn't get to have his perch for dinner last night and when Lilly brought his cup of cocoa, he asked her, "Mommy, can I still have my fish for supper tonight?"

"Of course you can, Johnny."

Johnny smiled brightly at his mother. She roughed up his hair and returned to her work. Johnny finished his breakfast and went to take care of Trouble. He later found his friends and played with them all day.

When it was time for dinner, Johnny and Lilly walked together to the lodge and Johnny ordered his perch from Rudy.

Rudy smiled broadly and said, "That is going to be a very special dinner, Johnny. Would you like a rice pilaf with that?"

"What is that?" Johnny asked Rudy.

"It is rice with chopped vegetables and nuts. It would be very good with your catch. I highly recommend it."

Johnny said, "Rudy, I will go with your advice."

"Excellent!" Rudy said, and then he took Lilly's order.

Finding a Home

   Rudy brought Johnny's perch out whole, on a bed of pilaf. It made for a very impressive presentation. Johnny insisted that his mother try it. He decided that perch was his favorite fish.

Chapter 4

The weekdays passed by and soon it was Saturday morning. Lilly went to work as usual and Johnny spent most of the day with Trouble. He walked the dog through the meadow and beyond the trees. Trouble perked up his ears and wagged his tail. "So, you hear them on the hill, do you?" Johnny said to the dog. Johnny could not hear them yet, but he knew that is why Trouble was wagging his tail. And soon, sure enough, even Johnny could hear the children squealing in delight, as they sailed down the grassy slope. Johnny and Trouble stepped out into the clearing. All the chatter and squeals ceased for a moment and then, all of a sudden, the children were all talking at once and pointing down the hill at Johnny and Trouble. One by one, they slid down the hill on their cardboard and joined Johnny and the dog at the bottom.

Leslie hid behind Lester. "She's afraid of dogs," Lester announced, a little too loudly.

"Only big ones like that dog of Johnny's," Leslie said, in her own defense.

"All dogs, Leslie!" Lester said, mocking her.

"Trouble is a good dog," Johnny said.

"Then why is his name Trouble?" Donna wanted to know.

"Mr. Thornton wanted people to think that Trouble is a mean dog."

"Why?" Donna asked.

Johnny shrugged his shoulders and said, "I don't know."

Fred stepped up to Trouble and gave him an ear scratch. Trouble wagged his tail faster. "He likes that," Johnny said.

Finding a Home

"When is your friend going to come home?" Hazel asked Johnny.

"I don't know. Soon I hope. He thanked me when I got to see him yesterday, for saving his life."

Hazel stepped closer to Johnny's side, looked at him with admiration and said, "You are a hero, Johnny."

"That is what everyone keeps telling me, but Trouble helped me."

"He is a smart dog?" Bobby asked.

"He is the smartest dog that I've ever seen," Johnny replied.

Hazel held her hand out in front of Trouble. Trouble sniffed her hand and then licked it. Hazel giggled and said, "That tickled!"

Johnny smiled at her and said, "He likes you." We both like you, he thought. She smiled sweetly back at him and he was sure that she could read his mind. He blushed and didn't know what was happening to him. She was just so different from all the other girls. He just couldn't sort it all out.

"You didn't bring your sled?" Bobby asked.

"No, I just thought that I would spend the day with Trouble. He is so lonely."

"You arc so nice, Johnny," Hazel said.

Fred rolled his eyes and said, "You can double up with some of us if you want to."

"You can't just turn that dog loose!" Lester shrieked.

"I thought Leslie was the one afraid of dogs, Lester?" Fred taunted him.

"I was just thinking of Leslie!" Lester retorted.

"Sure you were," Bobby said.

"He will be fine," Johnny said. "He will stay right here with us." Johnny untied his leash and they all walked up the hill together.

Hazel was the first one to go down the hill. "Come on Johnny, you can ride down the hill with me, if you want to?" Johnny looked around him in confusion. He wanted to so badly, but did he dare? "Well, are you coming or not?" There was his answer. He sprinted for Hazel and her sled. Fred smiled, knowingly. Hazel and Johnny went flying down the hill, with Trouble running right beside them, barking happily. Hazel's ringlets danced behind her and tickled Johnny's face. Johnny was very happy. When they landed at the bottom of the hill, Johnny stood up and Hazel extended her hand to him. He pulled her up from the sled. Her green eyes sparkled above her rosy cheeks. He had never seen anything so pretty.

She broke the spell and said, "Come on, you grab the other end."

Johnny picked up his end of the sled and the three of them raced back up the hill. Each time they rode down on their sled, Trouble raced along the side of them. Trouble stuck by Johnny's side the whole time, even without his leash. Soon, all the children felt comfortable with the dog being around them. By the end of the day, Trouble's tongue was hanging out the side of his mouth, but he still wagged his tail enthusiastically. When it was time for Johnny to head back home, he tied the leash back on Trouble and said goodbye to all his friends. Johnny returned Trouble to his dog house and fed and watered him, and then he went home. When he stepped into the cabin, he was surprised to see that his mother was already there. She was in the bathroom, wearing a pale pink slip and fussing with her hair. She had it all piled onto the top of her head. Loose curls hung down the back of her neck. "I've never seen you wear your hair like that before," Johnny said.

"Oh, I just thought that I would try something new. Do you like it like this?"

"It is alright, I guess. You look pretty no matter how you wear your hair."

She bent down and planted a kiss on the side of his cheek. "You are my best admirer."

"Mr. Thornton and I are your best admirers. Did you know that he wants Doc to hire nurses that look like you?"

Lilly threw back her head and laughed. "Are you serious? Did he really tell Doc that?"

"Doc told me himself just this morning, at the lodge."

"That old man is just too funny."

"See, I knew that you would like him, when you got to know him."

Lilly smiled at him and went back to messing with her hair. She held bobby pins between her lips, tucked a small ribbon bow into the mix of curls and pinned it securely. Lilly then took her nicest dress from a hanger on the back of the bathroom door and stepped into the dress. She buttoned all the tiny buttons and tied the bright pink sash round her waist. "Are you excited about getting to go over to Molly's house tonight?"

"I don't know."

"She said that, when I get you back, you are going to be spoiled rotten."

Johnny simply shrugged. He could not envision himself acting like Leslie, ever.

Lilly looked at her watch and said, "Doc will be here any moment."

"What about dinner?"

"You get to have dinner with Molly and her family. I hear that she is a really good cook."

"As good as you are?"

"Oh, I'm sure that she can cook every bit as good as me, if not better. She told me that her girls have made you something really special for dessert tonight." Soon, there was a light rap on the door.

Johnny opened the door. Doc stood before them in a suit and tie. Lilly's mouth dropped. She could not help it, he was so handsome.

Doc stood speechless on the front porch, in awe of how beautiful Lilly was, with her hair pinned up in soft curls. Johnny stood holding the door between the two adults. "Well, is he coming in or are we going out?" Johnny said.

"Oh, Doc, I'm so sorry. I just forgot my manners there for a moment," Lilly said, blushing.

"It's no matter. We can go ahead and set out, if you wish?"

"That is fine. I think we are ready to go."

Doc opened the passenger door for them. He pulled back the front seat so that Johnny could climb onto the tiny back seat. "Is there enough room for you back there, Johnny?"

Johnny looked around himself at the slanted roof line, which was just tall enough that his head didn't touch it. "Yeah, this is fine, Doc."

Doc repositioned the seat so that Lilly could sit down in the front of the car. He closed her door for her, climbed in behind the wheel and cranked over the engine.

Johnny peered over the two adults' shoulders at the dashboard of the car. "This is a fancy car, Doc."

"I can see that, even at your tender, young age, you have good taste," Doc replied.

"Is this a race car?" Johnny wanted to know.

"It probably could be, if I didn't have so much responsibility."

"I don't know what that all means?"

"You will, Johnny, all in due time," Doc said.

Johnny just shrugged his shoulders, leaned back in his seat and felt the rumble of the car beneath him. Soon, the car pulled up in front of Molly's house. Molly opened the front door of her house, even before they were all out of the car. Two teenage girls stepped out on the big front porch with their mother. They both had really long, flaming red hair.

"Oh my, Molly, your girls are stunningly beautiful," Lilly said, as she approached the house with Johnny.

One of the girls said softly, "Daddy says that we look like Momma, when she was young."

The other girl, the older one, stepped down from the porch and reached for Johnny's hand. Johnny instinctively stepped behind his mother, just out of reach of the girl with the flaming red hair.

"Oh give the little lad some room and a chance to get to know you, Holly," her mother told her. Reluctantly, Holly stepped back. "He is a wee bit shy, but he warms up to you in a hurry." Molly stepped down beside her daughter and reached for Johnny's hand. Johnny let Molly take his hand.

Lilly leaned down and planted a big kiss on his cheek. "You have a good time, and make sure to use your manners. Molly thanks so much."

"Don't mention it. We will be delighted to take care of this chap for you."

Lilly smiled, "You are a good friend, Miss Molly."

"You both deserve a nice evening out. Now go and enjoy yourself."

When Lilly and Doc returned from their evening out Lilly said to Molly, "I sure do appreciate you watching Johnny."

"Anytime, my dear, having Johnny was a pleasure. The girls said that anytime you need a sitter, let them know."

"Tell them thanks for me. I will be happy to take them up on that."

"So, did you have a good time at Molly's house?" Lilly asked Johnny, over the rumble of the car engine.

"I sure did. Did you know they have a cat?"

"I did not know that."

"They sure do. Its name is Whiskers and it is really fluffy."

The next morning, Lilly said to Johnny, "What do you say that we take Trouble for a walk?"

Johnny brightened up and said, "That is a terrific idea!"

Together, they walked the dog through the meadow. A light breeze had picked up and the tree tops swayed ever so slightly. The breeze felt good, Johnny felt good, and the birds were singing.

 After their walk Johnny asked his mother, "Can I go see Mr. Thornton now? We have so much to catch up on."

Lilly smiled and said, "Ok, let's go!"

When they arrived at the hospital, Lilly said, "Remember, Johnny, we can't stay long, because your friend is still weak.

 "Okay," Johnny said, and the two of them walked into Mr. Thornton's room together.

 "I told you to leave him at home and just come see me by yourself!" Mr. Thornton said to Lilly.

 "Hello, Mr. Thornton, I'm glad to see that you are feeling well," Lilly said.

 "Boy oh boy, do I have a lot to tell you!" Johnny said to Mr. Thornton.

 Mr. Thornton replied, "I was afraid that you were going to say that."

 Just then there was a light tap on the door and Doc entered the room. "I'm sorry to intrude folks, but Hank was brought in last night by Tony."

Finding a Home

Lilly was the first to speak from their group, "What is wrong? Is he alright?"

Chapter 5

"We are running tests on him. He is in and out of consciousness and has a very high fever. He keeps calling for you Lilly. Could you sit with him for a bit and talk to him. I just thought that perhaps it will help calm him down. He is delirious. I can have one of the nurses keep an eye on Johnny while he visits with Mr. Thornton."

"Johnny you be a good boy and I will be back just as soon as I can." Johnny looked at his mother and nodded. He knew that this sounded bad and he was very concerned for his friend Hank. He watched his mother follow Doc out of the room.

Doc headed down the long corridor and Lilly followed him; they passed the nurse's station and walked into a room right next to it. Lilly's heart sank at the sight of Hank lying on the hospital bed, surrounded by blinking monitors and IVs. An oxygen mask covered his mouth and nose. Doc motioned to a chair beside the bed and Lilly nodded and sat down. She looked over at Doc and then reached for Hank's nearest hand and covered it in both of her own. His hand lay limp within her hands.

Doc said, "Let me know if you need anything. The nurses are closely monitoring him, as I am myself."

"Thank you, Mark."

Doc nodded and left the room. Lilly let Hank's hand rest in her own and gently rubbed the top of his hand with her other one. Minutes ticked by on the wall clock and then Hank started to mumble and soon he thrashed his head back and forth and screamed for Tony over and over again, and then he called out to her, "Hold me, Lilly. Hold me up."

She leaned closer to him and said in a low voice, "I've got you, Hank."

"Don't let me go," he mumbled.

A tear slipped down her cheek and she said, "I will never let you go."

Hank settled back down and seemed to sleep comfortably for a while. Lilly leaned back in her chair with Hank's hand in her lap and closed her eyes. It felt good to feel the warmth of his hand in hers. It felt good to just be here next to him. She sat back up when she felt him start to thrash about again.

Doc was just about to reenter the room and stopped just inside the doorway. He saw the same thing; Hank was screaming for Tony. He was telling Tony to hold on, to keep his legs out of the water, and not to get wet. Then he said, "The mermaid is holding me up, she has me." Then, to Lilly's surprise, his eyes flew open wide. Hank blinked wildly and tried to focus and he lowered his voice as he said, "Lilly, you are a mermaid."

"What?" Lilly asked.

"You were there, Lilly. You would not let me sink. You made me keep fighting. I'm alive because of you. You were all I could think of out there. You are the mermaid. You are my mermaid," he whispered, and then closed his eyes. Lilly leaned forward and laid her head next to him on the bed and wept. Doc was concerned because Hank was still delirious. He stepped quietly from the room. Lilly never knew that he was there.

Lilly felt someone gently nudge her on the shoulder, she lifted her head and Hank swept her up into his arms and kissed her full on the lips.

Hank said, "I've wanted to do that since the first time I ever laid eyes on you. Lilly, I love you, with all my heart and soul."

Lilly threw herself into his arms. He kissed her and held her close. Their hearts pounded against the chest of one another. A nurse walked into the room and smiled broadly at the two of them, as they pulled apart from their embrace. Lilly blushed.

"Well, I see that you have made an amazing recovery, Hank," the nurse said cheerfully.

Lilly said, "I need to go and see if Mr. Thornton has had enough of Johnny yet." Hank reluctantly let go of her hand. She got up and walked down the hall.

When she walked into Mr. Thornton's room, he said to her, "There you are, at last! I thought you had forgotten this chap here. I thought that I had died already and was sent to hell, and this was my punishment for all eternity."

Johnny laughed and said, "Mr. Thornton, you are so funny."

"See that! He thinks I'm kidding."

Johnny asked, "How is Hank, Mommy?"

Lilly smiled at them both and said, "It looks like Hank is over the worst of it."

Mr. Thornton said, "Those young ones spring back much quicker. I'm glad for your friend. He sounds like a fine chap. Doc is going to keep me here until hell freezes over."

Johnny said, "He wants to make sure that you are all better!"

"Bah, they just want to squeeze the last penny out of me while they still can."

"Hey, I know," Johnny said, "maybe Hank will let Mr. Thornton go fishing with us?"

"Have you completely lost all your marbles?" Mr. Thornton said.

"Huh?" Johnny responded.

"No sir, I'm a land lover. I made my living logging. Land and trees, they are for me."

"You don't like to fish?" Johnny asked disappointedly.

"Did I say anything about not liking to fish? Of course I like to fish, what man doesn't like to fish?" Johnny simply shrugged his tiny shoulders. "I do all my fishing from the land. Well, sometimes from the pier, but you will never see me on a boat. No sir, not me!"

Johnny and Lilly left and returned the next day to visit their two friends. Lilly was just dropping Johnny off in Mr. Thornton's room when Hank appeared in the doorway. "Excuse me, folks, for barging in, but it seems that my ride to the hospital did not stick around to drive me home."

"I'll be happy to give you a lift home, Hank," Lilly said. "Mr. Thornton, this is Hank, he is the man we have been telling you about."

Hank stepped up to Mr. Thornton's bed and shook his hand. "I'm very pleased to meet you, sir," Hank said.

"Have your ears been burning? I'm surprised to see that you still have those two ears. That's all I've been hearing about is Hank this and Hank that from these two."

Hank smiled broadly and said, "I hope it was all good."

"Good! You've practically been elevated to sainthood by these two."

Lilly spoke up, "Now, Mr. Thornton, I wouldn't go that far."

"Okay, maybe I did exaggerate a little bit."

Hank laughed and said, "In any case, I think I'm in good company."

Mr. Thornton said, "Hank, you can drive Lilly's car, and take that kid with you. It will be fine with me if you leave Lilly here."

"That is real gentlemanly of you, Mr. Thornton," Hank said, "but Lilly is coming with me."

"If I was still a young buck, you wouldn't be getting away with her."

Hank smiled warmly at him and said, "It appears that I have a lot of lucky stars to thank."

"You bet you do," Mr. Thornton said.

35

"I'll come and see you again just as soon as I can, okay Mr. Thornton?" Johnny said.

"Okay, just be sure to bring your momma."

They left the hospital and Hank gave Lilly directions to his house. Lilly turned onto a little tree lined country lane. There were no other houses along the way. At the end of the long narrow lane sat a two story house, tucked into a grove of pines. Lilly pulled up in front of it and stopped her car.

Hank said, "There she is, home sweet home."

"Hank, that is beautiful," Lilly said.

Johnny exclaimed, "Wow! That looks kind of like a big ship."

"It does," Lilly said, "I've never seen anything like that."

Hank laughed and said, "This is the house that I grew up in. The grandfather of the gentleman that my folks bought it from was one of the first ship builders to settle here in Fort Bragg."

"He built it himself?" Lilly asked.

"Yes, he did, he built what he knew. The veranda is kind of a stand in for the deck, I guess but, in general, it is designed after the old galleons," Hank said.

"Can we go inside?" Johnny asked.

"Sure," Hank said, "It was built in the mid-1800's."

"No, we can't go in today," Lilly said, "Hank has been through a lot, Johnny."

She looked at Hank and smiled softly. "Another time we could, perhaps?"

Hank grinned and said, "Most definitely, do you promise?"

Still smiling she answered, "I promise."

"Okay, I will hold you to that!" Hank said, and reluctantly got out of the car. He walked past his pickup and smiled. The last time he had seen the pickup was at the harbor. He stopped at his door and took down a note that had been taped there. He turned around and watched as Lilly pulled out of the driveway. Johnny was still in the back seat and was waving goodbye to him. Hank gave him a high, long sweeping wave. With a sudden feeling of loneliness, he watched the car recede into the distance, until there was nothing but a plume of dust.

He looked down at the note in his hand; it was from Tony. Tony and his family had brought his truck home for him and had left a pot of stew in the refrigerator. They would be by in a few days to bring him more food and fresh baked bread. He smiled and thought to himself, that's Italians for you, they are wonderful people. He opened the door and stepped inside. Somehow, the house was not the same. He just stood in the still open doorway for a few moments, adjusting his eyes to the dimly lit interior. It looked the same and nothing had changed in the house, but then it hit him. It was him, he was forever changed. The house was empty, yet it was no different than it had been for years, ever since his parents had passed away. He realized that it wasn't just the house that was empty, it was his life. He had thought he had it all. He thought he was happy, until Lilly and Johnny walked into his life. He had thought nothing was missing, but now he knew that he was wrong about that. He shook his head in amazement and said to the empty walls, "So this is what love feels like. Dang, it feels good!"

While Lilly was driving back home from Hank's house, she came to terms with her new situation. She was in love with Hank and it felt wonderful.

The next afternoon Lilly took Johnny to the hospital to see Mr. Thornton. They started to walk past Emily's desk, but she called out to them. "Your friend, Mr. Thornton, has been moved to the elder care facility here in town, Pine Crest."

"Oh, we had no idea," Lilly said.

"Doc felt that he is doing well enough to move over there, but he is still very weak. He fussed about going back home, but Doc told him that is out of the question, for right now anyway," Emily said. "Do you know where Pine Crest is located? I can give you directions."

Lilly said, "I have driven past it a few times. Thank you Emily, we will head over there now."

Johnny and Lilly stepped out of the car at Pine Crest. The grounds were meticulously maintained. Pine Crest was a single story complex of four buildings, which boxed in a huge courtyard. When Johnny and Lilly stepped through the entrance door, they could see pretty striped umbrellas over tables out in the courtyard, just beyond the receptionist's desk. There were some elderly people sitting around a few of the tables chatting with one another. Some sat in wheelchairs that had been rolled up to the tables, while others were in normal chairs.

"Hello, may I help you?" the receptionist asked.

Lilly's gaze fell to the young woman sitting behind the desk. "Yes, please, we are here to see Mr. Thornton."

"Let me see." The young woman glanced down at a chart on her desk. "Oh, here he is. He is a new arrival, he just came in yesterday. It says that he is in room 14B. May I please have the two of you sign in on our visitor's log?" she asked, and slid yet another chart across her desk toward Lilly.

"Do you have a pen?" Lilly asked.

The receptionist blushed and said, "Of course," as she fumbled through her desk drawer, "here somewhere." She finally produced a pen and handed it to Lilly, beaming a bright smile.

Lilly smiled back and took the pen from her. "Thank you." Lilly signed in for both her and Johnny.

The receptionist slid her chair back away from her desk and said, "I will be happy to show you the way to his room. It is down this way on the south wing." She motioned with a wave of one of her slender arms towards a long corridor. "Follow me, please. Are you family members?"

Johnny said proudly, "We're friends of his."

"Is that so? Well he will be happy to see you, I'm sure."

"He likes it when I bring my mommy with me. He said so."

"Did he, now?" The receptionist asked and shot Lilly a knowing glance. She said to Johnny, "Your friend is a flirt, I take it?"

Johnny looked up at Lilly, confused. Lilly answered for Johnny, "Yes, of the first degree," Lilly said smiling.

"Well, in here, a pretty face can make their day and these little old ladies act like high school girls, when Doc makes his rounds. It is so cute to see them, they fall all over him." She stopped in front of a closed door and said, "Here we are, 14B." She rapped softly on the door.

"What do you want?" A gruff voice said from the other side of the door.

"Mr. Thornton, you have visitors."

"Well, what are you waiting for? Bring them in."

The young woman tentatively opened the door and stepped inside. Johnny and Lilly followed her. She walked up beside his bed, extended her small hand to him and said, "Mr. Thornton, welcome to Pine Crest. I'm Amanda."

Mr. Thornton took her hand and gave it an affectionate squeeze. "Amanda, I'm happy to see you. I thought that they only had homely nurses in this whole dang town."

"I'm the receptionist."

"Well you can stop in anytime you like."

"That is very kind of you, Mr. Thornton. Now, if all of you will excuse me, I need to get back to my desk." She hesitated and said to Lilly, "I'm sorry that I didn't properly introduce myself earlier. I'm Amanda." She held her hand out to Lilly.

Lilly shook her hand and said, "I'm Lilly and this is my boy, Johnny."

"I expect that I will be seeing quite a bit of the two of you then?"

Johnny said, "I will be here every time I can get Mommy to bring me. Mr. Thornton is my best friend."

Mr. Thornton thought for a moment and said in a sad voice, "Johnny is my only friend."

Amanda thought what an odd pairing of friends. She simply smiled and said, "I really need to get back. Please excuse me." With that said, she turned and left them.

"I told Doc that I wanted to go back home, but he wouldn't let me. He is a stubborn cuss for his age."

Lilly smiled and said, "I'm sure that he would say the exact same thing about you."

Johnny chimed in and said, "And Doc would be right."

"Hey, I just called you my only friend."

Chapter 6

"I'm proud to be yours and that is true. I'm just telling you straight up, man-to-man like." -Lilly giggled, she could not help herself.

"I hate the food here! They will not let me have anything fried. You're a southern girl, Lilly; you know everything tastes better fried."

"Mommy makes the best fried chicken!"

"I just bet that she does. Maybe the two of you could sneak me a little piece of it in here?"

"I'm afraid we can't do that," Lilly said gently, "Doc knows what is best for you."

"I could starve to death in a place like this!"

Lilly moved closer to his bedside, rested a hand upon his arm, and said, "Now you and I both know that is not going to happen. You have to eat what they bring you, so you can build up your strength. Once you build up your strength, you will be able to get released from here."

"Has Doc been coaching you?" Mr. Thornton asked her.

"No, why would you think a thing like that?"

"You sound just like him, almost word for word."

"He went to school for a long time and, from what I understand, learned even more from his father. I heard that they practiced together for quite some time," Lilly said.

Mr. Thornton said, "Yeah, Doc senior was my doctor when the kid was still in diapers." Lilly smiled at the thought.

Johnny said, "When you get strong enough, you can go for a walk with Trouble and me. We would like that, Mr. Thornton."

"Me too, Johnny, I would like that too."

Johnny saw tears welling up in Mr. Thornton's eyes. "Don't be sad, Mr. Thornton, we will get you home soon."

"I'm just plumb tuckered out," he said, with tears leaking from his eyes.

"Johnny, I think that we should let Mr. Thornton get some rest."

Johnny stepped up next to him and affectionately rubbed his arm. "I will come back and see you just as soon as I can, okay?"

"Okay, you do that. I just need to rest right now." Reluctantly, Johnny turned away from his friend and followed his mother out of the room.

When Johnny returned home with his mother, he walked up the road to take care of Trouble. As usual, Trouble wagged his tail and jumped up and down in delight at the sight of Johnny. Johnny walked over to Trouble and kneeled beside him. He wrapped his little arms around Trouble, buried his face into Troubles neck and wept. "I'm worried about Mr. Thornton, Trouble, he didn't look so good when I saw him today," Johnny sobbed. "We just can't lose him. I just can't bear to lose him." Johnny's whole body quaked with sobs. Trouble pulled back from Johnny and licked the tears from his face, and then he lay down next to where Johnny kneeled. "You're the best buddy ever, Trouble, because you understand so many things." Trouble looked up with his soft brown eyes, and slowly wagged his tail. Johnny lay down next to the dog and snuggled up to him and fell fast asleep.

That is how Lilly found them when she came looking for Johnny, because it was time for them to go to the lodge for dinner. It was a heartwarming sight to see her little boy lying there like that, with the dog that was twice his size. She always knew that he was safe with that dog; those two loved each other. Trouble lifted his head as she approached and licked Johnny's face to wake him. Lilly smiled and said to the dog, "You're such a good boy, Trouble."

Johnny blinked his eyes a couple of times, trying to get his bearings. When he figured out where he was, he looked sheepishly up at his mother. "I guess I fell asleep."

"That is how I found you. You and Trouble were sound asleep together. It is time for us to go get some dinner." Johnny got up off the ground and together they walked to the lodge.

As soon as they sat down at the table in the back of the kitchen, Lou approached them. "Lilly, a letter came for you in today's mail," Lou said, as he handed her an envelope.

"Thank you, Lou."

"You are certainly welcome," Lou said, and walked away."

"Who is it from?" Johnny wanted to know.

Lilly looked at the envelope and was delighted to see that it was from Beth. "It is from Beth." Eagerly, Lilly opened it. As she read the letter, her delight slipped from her face, and it was replaced by sorrow.

Johnny saw his mother's face change and he asked her, "What does it say, Mommy?"

A tear slipped from Lilly's eyes and she said, "Grandpa has gone to heaven."

"Beth also said that Mrs. Bailey is not doing so well now. Beth is spending a lot of time nursing her and helping her out with her house." Lilly knew that once Mrs. Bailey passed, Beth and her family could be out of work. The very next day, Lilly approached Lou and told him the sad news about Grandpa passing away.

Lou said, "We have all lost a good friend, who was a great man."

Lilly said, "I'm worried about my friend Beth and her family. Lou, I know that you have been talking about the possibility of hiring a new cook on the dinner shift."

"That is true, Lilly. Lately, we seem to be getting more business than we can handle. So far, we do not have any unhappy clients, but I worry that day may be coming. Word of mouth is everything to a business like mine."

"Beth is a much better cook than I am and you have never seen a harder working couple than Beth and her husband."

Lou could not help but to smile at Lilly. "So, let me see, Lilly, if I have this right? You are not just asking me to give your friend Beth a job, but her husband too? I might be looking to hire one cook, but not two."

"Buster is very handy. He can fix just about anything that you can throw at him."

"Lilly, I already have David helping me to do that. Well, he can fix most things anyway, and the rest I hire out."

"What about the things you hire out? I bet Buster could fix those."

"You sure know how to back a man into a corner."

"I don't mean you any disrespect, Lou, but these are just really good people. They take so much pride in anything that they do."

"Okay, Lilly, this is what I can do. I will offer the same deal to Beth that I have offered to you. For Buster, I can only offer him part time work for now, but it will be with pay." Lilly threw her arms around Lou and kissed his cheek. Lou was astonished, but kept his composure and simply said, "You are welcome."

"So, I can write them and tell them today?"

"You may do so."

"Oh, I can't wait to tell Johnny!"

"I will inform Howard and David that help will soon be on the way. I'm sure that will be welcome news to the both of them," Lou said.

When Johnny came in for his lunch that day, Lilly told him the news. Johnny was ecstatic. He could not wait until he was finished with his lunch, so he could tell all his new friends the wonderful news. He wolfed down his lunch, ran up the lane to get Trouble, and then set off for the grassy hill with his sled. When he reached the hill, to his disappointment, there was no one there. He sat his sled on top of the hill and, with Trouble by his side; he entered the woods by the well-worn trail on the other side. The birds were singing in the tree tops until a blue jay squawked loudly, announcing the presence of Johnny and Trouble. Suddenly, all fell silent, but then, in the distance, Johnny could faintly make out the sound of his friends approaching. "Come on, boy," Johnny said to Trouble, and broke into a run down the path to meet them.

When Johnny caught sight of them, he stopped running, put a hand on each leg and was panting so hard he could barely get the words out when they came within hearing distance. "My friends are coming to Fort Bragg!"

Leslie was the first one to respond to him. "What are you talking about?"

"My friends from Texas are coming here!" Johnny panted.

Fred said, "Your two buddies, Robert and James, right?"

Johnny looked at Fred and grinned broadly, shaking his head yes.

"Johnny, I'm so happy for you," Hazel said, stepping out of the group and fondly running her slender fingers over Trouble's back.

"Lou is going to give their parents jobs so now they can move here."

"Are they nice?" Donna was anxious to know.

"Of course they are nice." Bobby answered the question for Johnny. "They are his friends, aren't they?" Donna shrugged meekly.

"You will really like them, Donna, they are a lot of fun," Johnny told her enthusiastically.

"When are they going to get here?" Fred asked.

"I'm not sure yet, my mom said that she is going to write to them tonight."

"So, you don't know if they're coming yet?" Leslie said snidely.

The joy fell from Johnny's face and he said, "No, I don't know for sure yet."

Bobby stepped out of the group, stood next to Hazel and said, "Well, sure they are going to come, Johnny. Why wouldn't they?"

"Grownups sometimes get funny notions that us kids just can't understand," Johnny said sadly. Almost all the children in the group shook their heads in agreement with Johnny.

"Come on, the last one to the hill is a rotten egg!" Fred called out, and sprinted ahead with his cardboard sled flapping beside him.

"No fair! He got a head start!" Leslie cried out.

"Don't be such a cry baby!" Lester told his sister, and then bolted after Fred.

"I'm telling!" Leslie shouted after him, as all the other children ran with him toward the hill. Leslie trailed along after them.

That evening, as soon as Lilly got off work, she sat down and penned the letter to Beth and her family. When Lilly was finished, she sealed the envelope and stood up. "Johnny, how would you like to go see Mr. Thornton this evening?"

"Wow, can we, Mom?"

"I would like to get this letter to the post office just as soon as I can. So, since we are going to be in town anyway, I thought that you would like to see your friend."

"I can't wait to tell him the good news about James and Robert! They are going to come here to Fort Bragg, aren't they, Mommy?"

"I can't see any reason why they would not want to, Johnny. There is nothing for them out there on those cotton fields. There is nothing to look forward to out there."

"Leslie said that they may not come," he told his mother sadly.

"Well, we shall hope that Leslie is wrong in this instance," Lilly said, and picked up her purse and slipped the letter inside. Then they got into the car and headed into town. Lilly first dropped the letter off at the post office and then they headed over to see Mr. Thornton. Johnny and Lilly walked into Mr. Thornton's room and was surprised to see him sitting in a wheelchair.

"You must be feeling better today?" Lilly said.

"No, they made me get out of bed and wheeled me out to the dining room for dinner."

"That must have been nice?" Lilly said cheerfully.

"They put me at a table with a bunch of old women."

"You can't make new friends if you never go out of your room," Johnny said.

"I don't need any new friends. The nurse said I needed to socialize, so I just went to make her stop nagging at me."

"My friends might be coming here from Texas," Johnny said happily.

"You mean those two rowdy youngsters that you keep going on about?" Mr. Thornton said.

"Yep," Johnny said, through a wide grin.

"I'm right happy for you, Johnny." Mr. Thornton cleared his throat and then added, "Johnny, how would you like to have that dog?"

Chapter 7

Johnny was confused, "But Trouble is your dog, Mr. Thornton. You love him and he loves you."

"Yes, Johnny, that is true, but he also loves you. I've got to think about what is best for Trouble. Doc says that he can't release me because I have no one at home to care for me. He says that it is doubtful that I will ever be ambulatory again."

"What does that mean?" Johnny asked.

Lilly spoke up and said, "Johnny, it means that Mr. Thornton can't walk."

"You can't walk?" Johnny asked, astonished.

"It was that darn stroke, Johnny, but I'm going to keep trying. I'm a fighter from way back. Never give up, Johnny. Always remember that; never give up. Well, do you want him or not?"

"Of course I want him," Johnny said, and then he looked at his mother hopefully.

"We will have to ask Lou if it is alright to keep Trouble at our cabin. The answer is really up to Lou."

"Lilly, would you carry a message for me to Lou?" Mr. Thornton asked.

"Yes, certainly I will."

"You tell your boss man that I will finally sell my place to him so that he can own that whole dang road. I will sell it to him on one condition and one condition only."

"What is that Mr. Thornton?" Lilly asked.

"He has been after me to sell my place to him for years. So now he can have it, but he has to let Johnny have the dog."

"I can't say that to my boss."

"Well then, you tell him to come and see me here and I will tell him straight up."

"All right, that I can tell him," Lilly said. "I will not mention the dog to him. We will just wait to see what he has to say about it."

"That is fair enough. Johnny, I think it is safe to say that the dog is almost as good as yours."

"I sure do hope so, Mr. Thornton. I will be good to him."

"I have no doubt about that, Johnny, because you already have been good to him, and you have been a good friend to me too. Now, go on, the two of you get out of here, I need some rest. Lilly, would you two find that nurse of mine on your way out and tell her that I need to get in my bed?"

"I will, Mr. Thornton, you have a good night," Lilly replied, and then she and Johnny left his room. Lilly inquired about the nurse at the receptionist's desk.

Amanda said, "I will find his nurse straight away."

"Thank you, Amanda," Lilly said, and led Johnny out to the car.

That evening, when Johnny and Lilly were having their dinner, Lilly talked to Lou. "Mr. Thornton would like you to stop by Pine Crest to talk to him about possibly buying his property."

Lou's brows furrowed, "That can't mean good news for Mr. Thornton."

Lilly responded, "Doc told him that he may never be ambulatory again and since he has no help at home, that he needs to stay at Pine Crest."

"Well, as much as I would like to have the property, it is under sad circumstances that I may be able to acquire it."

Johnny said cheerfully, "He is making new friends."

Lou's brows shot up in surprise. "I didn't take him for the friendly type."

"The nurse told him that he had to get out of his room to socialize, so she sat him at a table tonight for his dinner with some women," Lilly said.

Lou smiled knowingly and said, "That was Doc's doing, no doubt."

Lilly smiled and nodded in agreement and repeated his words, "No doubt."

"I can spare a few moments tomorrow to stop by to see him. Now, if the two of you will excuse me. I need to give them a hand at the bar," Lou said, and left them to finish their meal.

The next evening, when Johnny and Lilly were seated with their evening meal, Lou approached their table. Johnny crossed his fingers on both hands and when Lou started to speak; Johnny sucked in his breath and held it. "It looks like, Johnny, you have a dog!" Lou said, with a radiant smile.

Johnny jumped up out of his chair and jubilantly jumped up and down. "Oh, thank you, Mr. Lou, thank you!"

"You need to thank Mr. Thornton. He sure knows how to drive a hard bargain."

"Wow, my very own dog! I just can't believe it. I'm so happy," Johnny said, and hugged his mother. Lilly hugged him back and placed a kiss upon his brow.

Lou then turned to Lilly and said, "Mr. Thornton's place will be a good project to start your friend Buster on, if he and his wife accept my offer. It looks like he is going to have quite a bit of work, initially anyway."

"I know that he will be happy to have the work, Lou," Lilly replied.

"Just as I predicted, Howard and David were very pleased to hear that Buster and Beth may be joining our staff here at the lodge," Lou told her.

"They will fit right in, Lou, that I can assure you," Lilly said.

"I just wanted to give Johnny the good news. Enjoy your meal," Lou said, and walked away.

Lilly looked at Johnny and smiled. His face was radiant. "It looks like Trouble is moving to our cabin."

"Isn't it wonderful that Mr. Thornton and Lou are so nice?" Johnny said.

"It certainly is, Johnny. Now, all we have to do is figure out a way to get Trouble's dog house to our yard."

"Hank will help us, Mommy. I will ask him the next time I get to see him."

"Well, if you ask him, I'm pretty sure he will do it," Lilly said grinning.

Johnny did not have to wait long because the very next day, just as Lilly was walking up the road after work; Hank pulled his truck into her little yard. He parked and stepped out with a huge bouquet of flowers in his hand. He walked down the lane to meet her.

When Hank drew near to her, he extended the flowers to her and said, "This is for the prettiest mermaid that I know."

"What a lovely surprise, Hank, thank you."

"I would very much like it if you and Johnny would join me for dinner at my place tomorrow night."

"That is two lovely surprises in a row. We would love to."

Hank looked around and said, "Where is Johnny?"

"He is off with Trouble playing with his friends, but he should be back any moment now. He has some very happy news to share with you."

"Happy news is always good," Hank said, and then he pointed out to the meadow. "Look there is my little Captain now."

Lilly looked toward the meadow and could see Johnny and Trouble racing toward them.

"Hank," Johnny shouted, "I have wonderful news!"

"That is what your mother tells me."

"Trouble is my dog now! Mr. Thornton gave him to me and Lou said it is alright if we keep him in our yard."

"Johnny, that is great! You are very lucky; he is a fine dog. You can tell that he is a purebred just by looking at him."

"He sure is. Mr. Thornton said that he paid too much money for him. He said that Trouble turned out not to be worth it, but I think he is great!"

"I'm very happy for you and Trouble. It seems to me that Trouble is going to be very glad to have a proud owner like you."

Johnny then said to Hank, "I have a favor to ask of you, Hank."

"Sure, Johnny, what is it?"

"Trouble has a really big dog house that we need help moving out behind our cabin and Mommy said that, if I asked you, she was sure that you would help us."

Hank shot Lilly a grin and said, "She said that, did she?"

Johnny nodded and said, "Yes sir, she certainly did."

"Well, Johnny, in that case let's go move ourselves a dog house."

"Hank, give me one moment to put these flowers in some water," Lilly said.

"Take your time, Lilly. Johnny and I can handle the dog house."

"Just us guys, Hank?"

"That's right, Johnny. Stuff like this is men's work," Hank said, and winked at Lilly.

Johnny beamed proudly and said to Lilly, "Hank is right, it is men's work, Mom."

Hank walked over to his truck and opened the passenger door for Johnny. Johnny climbed up into the cab and Hank closed the door after him. He then turned to Lilly and said, "We will be right back."

"Thank you, Hank."

Trouble sat down on the ground next to Lilly and whimpered. Johnny cranked down the window and said to Hank, "What about Trouble?"

"I've got him covered," Hank said, and dropped down his tailgate. "Let's go, boy." Trouble happily wagged his tail and jumped up onto the bed of the truck. Together, the three of them drove up the road to the old Thornton place to retrieve the doghouse. It was not long before Lilly could see them coming back up road with Johnny and Trouble riding in the back of Hank's truck with the dog house. Johnny was standing on the bed of the truck with his head just visible behind the cab and right beside him was Trouble standing on his hind legs with his paws on the cab and head an inch higher then Johnny's.

Please write a review on Amazon or Goodreads. It will be greatly appreciated.

C. S. Crook

Other books in this series include:

Johnny's Reptile Adventure (Johnny's Adventure Book 1)
by C.S. Crook
Link: http://amzn.com/B00LDCEPQY

The Skipper's Captain (Johnny's Adventure Book 2)
by C.S. Crook
Link: http://amzn.com/B00LR89PSW

Johnny's Heroic Adventure (Johnny's Adventure Book 3)
by C.S. Crook
Link: http://amzn.com/B00MD7O2Y8

Finding a Home (Johnny's Adventure Book 4)
by C.S. Crook
Link: http://amzn.com/B00MDYI7EC

The Magic Wishbone (Johnny's Adventure Book 5)
by C.S. Crook
Link: http://amzn.com/1503278832

Johnny's Treasure Adventure (Johnny's Adventure Book 6)
by C.S. Crook
Link: http://amzn.com/B0159IY7AQ